Anna, Banana,

and the
Little Lost
Kitten

Anna, Banana,

and the
Little Lost
Kitten

Anica Mrose Rissi

ILLUSTRATED BY Meg Park

SIMON & SCHUSTER
BOOKS FOR YOUNG READERS
New York   London   Toronto   Sydney   New Delhi

SIMON & SCHUSTER BOOKS FOR YOUNG READERS
An imprint of Simon & Schuster Children's Publishing Division
1230 Avenue of the Americas, New York, New York 10020
This book is a work of fiction. Any references to historical events, real people, or real places are used fictitiously. Other names, characters, places, and events are products of the author's imagination, and any resemblance to actual events or places or persons, living or dead, is entirely coincidental.
Text copyright © 2017 by Anica Mrose Rissi
Illustrations copyright © 2017 by Meg Park
All rights reserved, including the right of reproduction in whole or in part in any form.
SIMON & SCHUSTER BOOKS FOR YOUNG READERS is a trademark of Simon & Schuster, Inc.
For information about special discounts for bulk purchases, please contact Simon & Schuster Special Sales at 1-866-506-1949 or business@simonandschuster.com.
The Simon & Schuster Speakers Bureau can bring authors to your live event. For more information or to book an event, contact the Simon & Schuster Speakers Bureau at 1-866-248-3049 or visit our website at www.simonspeakers.com.
Also available in a Simon & Schuster Books for Young Readers hardcover edition
Book design by Laurent Linn
The text for this book was set in Minister Std.
The illustrations for this book were rendered digitally.
Manufactured in the United States of America
0317 OFF
First Simon & Schuster Books for Young Readers paperback edition May 2017
2 4 6 8 10 9 7 5 3 1
CIP data for this book is available from the Library of Congress.
ISBN 978-1-4814-8669-9 (hc)
ISBN 978-1-4814-8671-2 (eBook)
ISBN 978-1-4814-8670-5 (pbk)

For Johanna, Lillian, and Julia
—A. M. R.

Anna, Banana,

and the
Little Lost
Kitten

Chapter One
Just My Luck

"Which one's worse, walking under a ladder or a black cat crossing your path?" I asked, hopping over a line in the sidewalk. Chuck and I were walking to school and playing the game where you're not supposed to step on any cracks.

"They're both bad luck," my brother said. "About the same amount. But you can cancel out bad luck with *good* luck by finding a penny or a four-leaf clover, or knocking on something made of wood—like your head," he teased. He tried to tap his knuckles against my skull but I dodged out of the way.

"Missed me! Ha-ha." I straightened my back-pack on my shoulders.

Chuck had been reading *The Big Book of Small Superstitions* for a report he'd be giving at school today, so now he was kind of an expert. I wasn't sure I believed in that stuff—I love animals, so seeing a cat of any color seemed like good luck to me—but I thought it was fun to hear about.

"Breaking a mirror is the worst one," Chuck said. "Then you have bad luck for seven whole years. You'd have to find a lot of pennies to make up for that."

"Whoa." I wondered if I could train Banana, my dog, to sniff out lucky pennies. With her help, I bet I could find enough extra luck to share with everyone in my family and my best friends, Sadie and Isabel, too. Though Banana was more interested in chasing squirrels and eating treats than she was in luck or money.

I followed Chuck around the corner, toward the Surely Shirley house. I call it the Surely Shirley house because it says SHIRLEY on the mailbox in big purple letters, and when I asked Dad why, he said, "Surely Shirley lives there," which made me giggle. I didn't know if Shirley was the person's first name or last. Maybe it was both. But I was pretty sure an old couple lived there. I had seen them out in the yard a few times. Most likely they were Mr. and Mrs. Shirley.

Banana and I loved walking by the Surely Shirley house. In spring, summer, and fall, colorful flowers bloomed in the garden. Fancy lights twinkled in the tree branches all winter long. The bird feeders attracted lots of sparrows and robins, and the shiny, purple gazing ball and dancing frog sculpture were like something out of a fairy tale. It was always the most cheerful-looking yard on the block.

But it wasn't like that today. Not at all.

Today the garden looked brown and wilted, like everything in it was feeling sad. Sharp-seeming bristles and extra-huge thorns reached out like they wanted to bite us. It reminded me of the witch in the book I'd been reading, and how everything near her lost all its color whenever she got angry. There weren't any witches around here, of course—I knew that spooky story was only make-believe—but I walked a bit faster anyway.

"Do you think the Shirleys moved away?" I asked.

Chuck shrugged. "I dunno. Why?"

"Because the house looks kind of creepy and abandoned, doesn't it?"

Before he could answer, I heard a howling shriek and a crash in the bushes, like an enormous creature was racing straight toward us. I screamed and jumped as something white—was it a ghost?—streaked past me, just inches in front of my feet. My heartbeat pounded in my ears like a drum. I grabbed on to Chuck for safety.

It took me a few seconds to realize Chuck was laughing. I dropped his arm and looked where he was pointing, in the direction the white thing had gone.

There it was, across the street: not a ghost or a monster or a terrible, ferocious beast. It was a tiny white kitten. His ears were pink and his fur was as puffy as a dandelion ready for its seeds to be blown. His whiskers twitched as he looked straight at me, then he slipped into a hedge and disappeared from sight. He was adorable, not scary.

My cheeks felt hot with embarrassment and relief. Chuck clutched his stomach and tried to catch his breath from laughing so hard. "You should have seen your face!" he said. He stretched his mouth and flailed his arms in what I guessed was supposed to be an impression of me.

"You jumped too," I said.

"Did not!"

"Did too." But we were both grinning. Now that I knew we were completely safe, I had to admit it had been pretty funny.

"C'mon, scaredy cat," Chuck said. He leaped over a crack. "We'd better get moving before more kittens attack."

Chapter Two
A Funny String of Events

By the time we got to school, my heart rate had slowed from a gallop to a trot, and Chuck had finally stopped snickering. I wished him good luck with his report, and ran to find Isabel and Sadie. They were right where I thought they'd be: near the fence behind the swings, practicing tricks for String Club.

String Club was a new thing our classmate Keisha had started when everyone got excited about the tricks she was doing with a loop of yarn in the cafeteria last month. She'd learned the string tricks from her cousin Mo, who'd learned them from a kid at his school, who'd learned them from a book. Everyone at the lunch table wanted to know how to do them too, so Keisha had showed us. Then more people wanted to learn, and soon it turned into a club that met every Tuesday and Thursday at recess. Anyone who was interested could learn and practice tricks. All you needed to join was a piece of yarn or string, and our teacher, Ms. Burland, had brought in a whole ball of it.

By now almost all the third-grade girls were in String Club, and half the boys, too. Sadie was club secretary, so she used a clipboard to keep track of who'd learned which tricks and what level everyone was at. Most of us in String Club were still level one, but Isabel had mastered so many tricks, she was already level two. So far only Keisha had reached level three.

Before String Club started I only knew how to do Cat's Cradle, but now I could do Jacob's Ladder, the Butterfly, Cup and Saucer, and Witch's Broom. I was also getting pretty good at Cutting Off the Fingers, a trick where the yarn loops around each finger and it looks like if you yank the loose end hard enough, your fingers could come right off—but of course they don't.

If you do it right, the string slips away, sliding through your fingers like magic. But if you do it wrong, the string won't budge, and your fingers get all tangled. I'd been practicing it at home over and over again with Banana. Cutting Off the Fingers was Banana's favorite string trick. Every time it worked, she thumped her tail on the floor like applause. She did that sometimes when it didn't work too.

"Look!" Sadie said, holding up her hands as I approached. The yarn in her fingers was stretched into a trick called Cat's Whiskers. She held the "whiskers" in front of her face and meowed.

"She did it all by herself this time," Isabel said. "I didn't help once."

"Cool! Way to go," I said. Sadie beamed. She had been struggling with that trick all week.

I pulled a loop of yellow string out of my backpack and twisted it through my fingers. "Speaking of whiskers, guess what happened to me this morning?" I launched into the story about my scare with the ghost kitten. My friends' eyes went wide as I acted out the way I'd shrieked and jumped, and they laughed as I played up how tiny and cute the kitten had been. We were all still giggling about it when the bell rang to call us inside for class.

We settled into our desks and quieted down when Ms. Burland clapped twice to start the day. As she handed back our spelling tests, Isabel slipped me a note. I unfolded the paper and grinned at what I saw. She'd drawn a tiny ghost kitten underneath the word "BOO."

Later, in the lunch line, Sadie made us giggle again by saying, *"Meeeeeeeeeeooowwwwwwww,"* in an eerie voice. Her hands floated through the air like little ghost paws.

Even the word of the day seemed to be in on the joke. The word was "heebie-jeebies": *a feeling of nervous fear.* I liked the silly-but-shivery sound of it.

The kitten probably wouldn't have scared me so much if I hadn't already had the heebie-jeebies from thinking about the witch in my book. I hoped we'd see the kitten again on the walk home, so I could get a better look at him and maybe even pat him. He looked so sweet and soft. I wondered what the Shirleys had named him.

When Chuck and I got to the Surely Shirley house after school, I stared at the witchy garden, but the kitten was nowhere to be seen. A cold breeze blew against my neck and rustled through the dead leaves, making me shiver. I wished my friends were there with me to help me feel braver.

I stepped closer to Chuck and reminded myself there was no reason to be scared. I clicked my tongue against the top of my mouth and called, "Here, kitty kitty!" but the kitty didn't come.

"Maybe it hasn't learned to speak English yet," Chuck said.

I rolled my eyes, but that reminded me of a funny joke. "What's smarter than a talking cat?" I asked.

Chuck looked at me. "What?"

"A spelling bee!" I answered.

"That's dopey," Chuck said, but he was laughing.

"Nope!" I said. "It's purrrrrfect." He reached out to swat my arm, so I ducked and broke into a run. I raced him all the way home, and won.

Chapter Three
A Tale of Two Tails

I burst in the front door of our house, almost out of breath. Banana was right there waiting for me. She barked and twirled in a circle at my feet, to say she was happy to see me. Her toenails clicked against the floor as she spun. It sounded like she was tap-dancing.

I dropped to my knees and kissed her on the snout. "I missed you too," I said. "And I've got a *lot* to tell you." Banana's ears perked up. She's always been a great listener.

I shrugged off my backpack and clipped on her leash, and we set off around the block. While we walked, I told her about the fluffy little kitten who had turned me into a scaredy cat, and how Sadie and Isabel hadn't laughed at me when I'd told them—they'd laughed *with* me, which made it all seem better, because that's what best friends do.

"It sounds silly now, but I really was terrified," I admitted to Banana. "It was almost as bad as the time Chuck convinced me there was a werewolf in Nana and Grumps's basement."

Banana froze. I smiled to reassure her and tugged at the leash. "Don't worry," I said. "There's no such thing as werewolves. Chuck made that up to fool me when I was little. The noise was just a furnace that growled because it was broken." But Banana wouldn't budge. Her whole body held stiff as she stared at something on the other side

of the road. I turned my head to look, and let out
a gasp. Banana had spotted the kitten!

"That's him!" I said.
Banana pressed back her
ears and pushed her nose
forward. She crouched
low to the ground

and crept toward the kitten, pulling me behind
her. I looked both ways and we crossed the road.
Banana was as focused and determined as when

she sees a squirrel or thinks I might drop a piece of cheese I'm eating. She really wanted to play with him.

The kitten stared at Banana and flicked his tail. Banana wagged hers eagerly. But as we got closer, the kitten arched his spine and puffed out his fur like he wanted us to think he was made of sharp needles instead of soft tufts. Banana wasn't fooled.

"Banana!" I yelped as she lunged toward the kitten. I pulled on the leash to stop her from reaching him. The kitten hissed, jumped out of the way, and ran off through the bushes. I saw one last glimpse of his skinny white tail, and then he was gone.

Banana sniffed the ground where the kitten had been, wagging her tail fast. I hadn't seen her so excited since the cookout last summer when Chuck dropped his whole hamburger and she got to it first. But even though Banana was thrilled, I was worried about how the kitten felt.

"Banana, you scared him!" I said. Her ears and tail drooped. "I know you didn't mean to. You just wanted to say hello. But the kitten doesn't know us yet. We have to approach him gently. It's not nice to charge at new friends." Banana nudged my leg with her nose to say she was sorry.

"It's okay," I said. "You'll do better next time. I'm still glad we saw him." But then I realized: We were nowhere near the Surely Shirley house, and the kitten had run off in the opposite direction. What was he doing so far from home?

Chapter Four
What If

"Maybe the kitten doesn't belong to the Shirleys after all," I said to Banana as we returned home. "But then, whose kitten is he?"

I couldn't help worrying about it. Even while I was doing my Roman numerals worksheet for math and practicing Cutting Off the Fingers for String Club and setting the table for dinner, the kitten was still on my mind. What if he was lost? Even wondering that made me want to hug Banana extra tight. Losing a pet would be terrible.

But when I told my parents, they didn't seem concerned. "I'm sure he knows his way home,"

Mom said. "Some cats like to wander pretty far."

"Even little tiny ones?" I asked.

"Sure," Dad said. "Cats are very independent."

Before I could say anything else, Chuck made a disgusting sound and I turned to see him slurping up a strand of spaghetti while balancing a meatball on his nose. "Charles!" Mom shouted as the meatball rolled off, falling straight into Banana's mouth. "The dinner table is not a playground!"

Chuck grinned and my parents frowned, and everyone seemed to forget about the kitten.

But Banana and I didn't forget. I took her outside again before bed and we squinted into the dark, wondering if the kitten was out there, scared and lost and alone. I didn't see any sign of him.

Maybe my parents were right. Maybe the kitten was curled up at home, dreaming about the day's big adventures. I hoped so.

I thought about walking to the Surely Shirley house to ask, and maybe I would have if Sadie and Isabel were with us, but Banana and I knew better than to knock on a stranger's door by ourselves—especially on a moonlit, windy night. We ran back inside and got ready for bed instead.

I crawled under the covers and took out

my book, while Banana settled into her basket beside my bed. The girl in the book walked deep into the forest, following the path she thought her missing brother had taken. She didn't know it was a trap that would lead her straight to the witch's lair. It was the scariest chapter yet.

When Mom came to tuck me in and said, "Lights out," I closed the book like I was supposed to, reached down to pat Banana good night, and shut my eyes. But falling asleep was impossible. The girl and the witch kept floating through my brain, mixing with thoughts of the kitten.

I grabbed my flashlight from its hiding spot under the bed, turned it on beneath the blankets, and reopened the book. I had to find out what happened next.

I wished I could turn the page to see what would happen with the kitten, too.

Chapter Five
Losing Sleep

I dragged myself out of bed, moving as slowly as the sloths in Isabel's new favorite video. Usually Banana and I were the first ones down to the kitchen on Saturdays, but today my parents had to call us three times for breakfast.

Last night, as I'd read my book under the covers and Banana snored in her basket, the story had gotten scarier and scarier. Reading it after bedtime while the house was all quiet and dark had started to seem like a bad idea, but I hadn't been able to stop.

I'd read and read, until my eyelids felt as heavy as the iron key the witch had used to lock the girl in the enchanted cage. I fell into a dream where I was running through the forest, trying to get to the girl and her brother. Suddenly the forest gave way to a garden, which looked as overgrown and neglected as the garden at the Surely Shirley house, but a thousand times larger and creepier. Thorns and bristles grabbed at my shirt as I ran through the mist. I thought I spotted the kitten, but he kept disappearing from where I'd seen him and reappearing someplace else, like a ghost. The witch was after me and time was running out, but I couldn't leave the garden without saving the kitten from danger. I knew I was the only one who could help him.

I must have called out in my sleep because the next thing I knew, Banana's warm, wet tongue was licking my face, urging me awake. When I

opened my eyes, Banana had her two front paws
up on my mattress and was nuzzling against me
to push away the bad dream.

I'd patted Banana's soft ears and warm fur, and instantly felt so much better. If there were ever a real witch or ghost in our house, I knew Banana would protect me. Even though she was just a little wiener dog, she always had my back.

Now, in the daylight, I scooped some kibble into Banana's dish and poured myself a bowl of Gorilla Grams with milk. I wondered if the little white kitten was eating breakfast somewhere too. Or maybe he was still in bed, fast asleep, like I wished I could be.

I yawned, careful to cover my mouth with my hand since that's good manners. Banana yawned too, and stretched out her legs under the table at my feet. She didn't even try to cover her mouth, but nobody minded. Good manners are different for dogs.

"Earth to Anna." Chuck waved his arm in front of my face. "I said, will you please pass the orange juice? Yeesh."

I blinked and reached for the juice carton.

"You sure look sleepy this morning, kiddo," Dad said. "You didn't stay up all night reading, did you?"

"No! Of course not," I said. Which, technically, was true. I hadn't stayed up *all* night, just for a few extra chapters.

"Well, finish your breakfast so we can get hopping. There's a lot to do before Sadie and Isabel come over," Dad said.

My friends were coming over! That gave me a shot of energy. We were planning to practice for String Club, but I bet they'd also help me look for the kitty.

"Who wants first spin on the chore wheel?" Mom asked, like spinning the wheel to choose a chore was some kind of special treat.

"She does." Chuck pointed at me. I didn't argue. I figured I might as well get it over with.

I flicked the spinner and it went round and round before landing on FOLD LAUNDRY. "Yes!" I cheered. Folding laundry was an easy chore. I had lucked out.

Chuck spun the wheel and groaned when it

landed on YARD WORK. Banana barked and wiggled like she was trying to tell me something. I realized she was right. "Trade you," I said to Chuck.

He narrowed his eyes with suspicion. "Why?" he asked.

I shrugged. "No reason. I just feel like being outside." Chuck stuck out his hand and we shook on it.

He didn't need to know what Banana and I really had in mind: Outside, we could keep an eye out for the kitten.

Chapter Six
Operation Catch the Kitten

By the time Isabel's Abuelita dropped Isabel and Sadie off at my house, I had cleaned my room, brushed Banana, and raked all the leaves from our yard into two piles, plus re-raked one of them after Banana and I had jumped in it. More importantly, I had spotted the kitten! Unfortunately, Banana had spotted him too, and as soon as they looked at each other, the kitten had run off.

I was more convinced than ever that the little white kitten was lost.

Sadie and Isabel were sure of it too. "There aren't any missing cat signs around the neighborhood, though," Isabel said. "If he belonged to someone, they'd be looking for him. He's probably a stray."

I hadn't even thought of that. "If that's true, then we really need to find him," I said. "The kitten needs a home!" Banana wiggled in agreement.

Sadie looked thoughtful. "Signs are a good idea," she said. "If we can't find him, we should make some. Then people will know to be on the lookout."

"I think we'll find him, though. We're a really good team," Isabel said.

"Plus, Banana can help!" Sadie added. "She can smell where the kitten went, and we'll follow his trail."

"Yes!" Isabel clapped her hands together and Banana bounced back and forth between her and Sadie, eager to be involved.

I shook my head. "I'm sorry, Banana, but you'll have to stay inside." Banana sighed and lay down on the floor. She knew it was true. "The kitten is afraid of her," I explained to my friends. "If he sees her, he'll run."

"That makes sense," Isabel said. "Mewsic doesn't really like dogs either. Or other cats, for that matter." Mewsic was Isabel's huge orange tabby cat. He was even bigger than Banana.

"So how are we going to find him?" Sadie asked.

"The kitten is probably hungry. If we put out some food, maybe he'll come to us," Isabel suggested.

"A saucer of milk!" Sadie said.

Isabel nodded. "That too." She turned to me. "I'm guessing you don't have any cat food here."

I shook my head. We only had people food and Banana's kibble. "We might have some tuna, though. Let's ask my dad."

We ran downstairs with Banana at our heels. Dad was at the grocery store, but Mom helped us find a slice of turkey we could use, and a shallow bowl for the milk. "But if you catch any cats, no bringing them inside. Your father is very allergic," she said.

"Okay," I agreed. That was disappointing, but I knew she was right. Once when Dad picked me up at Isabel's house, he started sneezing from cat allergies immediately after crossing the doorstep. But we still could play with the kitten outside. We just had to find him first.

Isabel held open the front door and I walked slowly toward it, trying not to spill the milk. "Stay, Banana," I said. She went to the window to watch us.

I set the bowl down in the grass near the sidewalk, and Sadie put the plate of turkey beside it. We looked around. No kitten.

"So we just wait for him to show up to eat the food and then . . . catch him?" Sadie asked.

We looked at Isabel. She thought for a second. "Mewsic loves taking naps in cardboard boxes. Do you have any, Anna? We could put a towel inside one to make him a cat bed. I bet he'll crawl right in."

"Good idea," I said, and ran to get a box from the garage. It was a good thing Isabel knew so much about cats. I was glad to have an expert on my team.

We set up the box near the turkey and milk, and folded an old beach towel inside. It looked like a nice, soft spot for a kitten. We grinned at each other, feeling pleased with our work. Surely the kitten would love it.

We sat on the stoop of my house to watch

and wait for the kitten to come by.

And waited.

And waited.

And waited.

Chapter Seven
Change of Plans

Sadie sighed, crossed her eyes, and dropped her head onto my shoulder, then squeezed her loop of yarn into a clump. We'd been sitting on the stoop for what felt like hours, but hadn't seen any sign of the kitten. For a while, I'd kept watch while Isabel taught Sadie a string trick called Open the Gate, but now the gate had been opened a million times and I could tell my friends were getting antsy. In truth, I was getting a little impatient too, but I couldn't give up on the kitten. "You know," Sadie said, "maybe we should go look for him instead of sitting here doing nothing."

That made me feel bad, like she was calling me boring, but Isabel perked right up. "Yeah! Let's walk around the block."

I bit my lip. "But what if he comes for the food while we're gone?"

"Then he'll be taking a nap in the box when we get back," Isabel said. "He's probably more likely to come while we're not here, actually, now that I think about it. He might know it's a trap if we're watching."

"So by walking away, we double our chances of finding him," Sadie said.

I wasn't sure about that math, but my friends were already standing, so I got up too. I didn't want to just sit there by myself. "Okay, let's go," I said.

We set off around the block, in the same direction Chuck and I went to get to school. Sadie

ducked to look under bushes. I stood on tiptoes to peek over fences and into yards. Isabel made a *psst-psst-psst* sound. That was how she called her cat, Mewsic, at home. We all tried to walk softly so our footsteps wouldn't scare the kitten away.

This was much more fun than sitting on the stoop, waiting. It felt like we were detectives out on a sneaky cat-finding mission. But the kitten was too good at hiding.

We turned left, down the street with the Surely Shirley house. "That's where I first saw him," I said as we drew closer. "Yesterday morning, when I got the heebie-jeebies."

Isabel craned her neck to see, but Sadie drew back. "It does look kind of haunted," she said.

I stepped toward the garden, looking for any signs of the kitten. Sadie grabbed my arm. "What was that?" she asked.

"What?" Isabel said.

"Shhh," Sadie warned. "*That*. Listen."

We listened, and this time I heard it: a muffled sound coming from inside the house, like the cry of a kitten, or perhaps even—

"Is it a ghost?" Sadie whispered.

Isabel shook her head slightly, but she didn't seem certain. She looked all tense, like how Banana gets right before someone turns on the vacuum: ready to bolt.

A dark cloud passed over the sun, casting the house and garden in shadow. "Look," Sadie said, and I saw it too—a curtain shifted in the second-floor window, and for a second I thought I saw a face looking out at us.

I blinked and when I looked again, the face—if it had even really been there at all—was gone.

"Let's go!" I said, and took off at a run. My friends were right behind me.

I didn't slow down until we'd turned onto the next street. I was nearly out of breath and my heart was pumping hard, but I felt more excitement than fear. "What do you think that was?" I asked. "Could that noise have been the kitten?"

Isabel tucked back some loose hair that had fallen from her braids. "It sounded more like someone was crying," she said.

"Did you see that face in the open window?" Sadie asked.

I shuddered, but Isabel shrugged. "Well, someone lives there, don't they? They probably heard us and looked out."

Being logical wasn't as fun as being scared, but I had to admit Isabel's explanations made sense. And I was glad my neighbors weren't ghosts.

Sadie looked relieved too. "Whatever the person's sad about, I hope she feels better soon."

"Me too," I said, and Isabel agreed. We rounded the corner back onto my street. When we reached my front yard, Sadie stopped short.

"The kitten!" she said. "He was here!"

Chapter Eight
Thinking Outside the Box

We ran over to the dishes and cat box. Sadie was right: The kitten had definitely been there. He'd eaten all the turkey and lapped up half the milk. The towel in the box had a kitten-size dent in it, and a few white hairs were stuck to the cloth. The kitten must have taken a cat nap after his snack.

But even though he'd been there, he had already disappeared. I dropped to the grass and put my head in my hands. "Oh no. We missed him!" I couldn't believe it. This was terrible. I'd had a chance to save him and I'd blown it. I should never have walked away from the stoop.

But Isabel was dancing around with delight. "No, Anna, this is good news!" she said.

I lifted my head. "It is?"

"Yes!" she said. Beside her, Sadie nodded, her eyes bright. I didn't know how they could be so upbeat.

"First of all, it's good that he's eaten. Didn't you say he was too skinny?" Sadie said.

"Yeah . . ." I supposed that was true.

"And now that he knows there's food here, he'll be coming back for more!" Isabel sounded triumphant.

"You think so?" I asked.

"I'm sure of it," Isabel said. "And he's much

more likely to trust someone who's fed him. So now when we do catch him, he'll be less scared and squirmy."

I nodded slowly. That did seem good. "I still wish we'd rescued him, though," I said.

"Me too," Isabel said, and I knew she meant it. "But this is the next best thing."

"It will be okay, Anna," Sadie said. "We'll find the kitten soon. This was a good first step."

"Let's go inside and ask Banana if she saw him," Isabel said.

"Yeah." Sadie stuck out both hands and pulled me up from the ground. "And then we can make some signs."

Chapter Nine
Hanging Around

I got out some markers, crayons, and construction paper, and we sat at the kitchen table and got to work. Sadie wrote LOST KITTEN in big letters at the top of ten pieces of paper. Isabel drew a picture of the kitten on each one, and I wrote my first name and phone number plus PLEASE CALL IF YOU SEE HIM at the bottom.

I faced toward the window the whole time we were working so I would see if the kitten appeared in my backyard. Banana kept looking out the window too, and a few times she even perked up her ears like she might have heard a noise. But when I ran outside to look, there was nothing there.

Chuck came into the kitchen carrying his baseball glove and wearing a rhinestoned cowboy hat he'd gotten from Nana and Grumps. "What are you guys doing?" he asked, leaning over Sadie's shoulder to look. I braced myself for him to make a rude comment, but he surprised me by saying, "Cool. Can I help?"

Isabel put down the white crayon she'd been using. "The posters are done. But you can help us hang them up."

Chuck let out a loud burp in response and grinned like he'd done something clever. I rolled my eyes and Banana flattened her ears, but Sadie giggled. Isabel just waited patiently for his real reply. "I'll get some masking tape," he said.

Isabel, Sadie, and I took half of the signs in one direction, while Chuck and Banana took the others. Soon they were taped up all over the areas where we thought the kitten might be.

LOST KITTEN

ANNA 555 - 6158
PLEASE CALL IF YOU
SEE HIM

I skipped back to the house alongside my friends, feeling hopeful. Everyone in the neighborhood would see the signs, and with that many people keeping an eye out for the kitten, we were sure to find him soon.

We went up to my room and got out our yarn loops, but there was only time to practice a few string tricks before Sadie's mom arrived to take her and Isabel home.

"Call us if there's any kitten news!" Sadie said as she climbed into the backseat of the car.

Isabel gave me a quick hug. "I'm sure he'll be back soon," she said. She hugged Banana, too, before following after Sadie.

I sat on the steps and waved to my friends as the car drove out of sight. Banana leaned over and licked my ear, making me laugh.

I was so lucky to have two best friends and a best Banana. They always made everything better. I hoped soon the little lost kitten would have someone to lean on too.

Chapter Ten
Spell It Out

That night and the next morning, Banana and I were on high alert, waiting for the phone to ring with news of the kitten. But no one called.

Dad let me put out some tuna at lunchtime and I waited at the window for the kitten to come eat it. I stopped watching for only a minute to Skype with Nana and Grumps, but when I got back, the tuna was gone. It was like Nana sometimes said: "A watched pot never boils."

I walked around the block looking for

him so many times that Mom finally said, "No more cat-searching until you've used each of your spelling and vocabulary words in a sentence."

I groaned and went to get a pen. Banana helped me write a story about a kitten who was so pale he looked almost *translucent*. Everyone thought he'd *transformed* into a ghost. But a girl *translated* his meows into words and *transcribed* them onto a piece of paper, and learned he wasn't a ghost, he was only hungry. So the girl gave him some food and he gave her a purr, and they were both pleased with that *transaction*. The girl invited the kitten to *transfer* his belongings to her house, and the kitten accepted, and they both lived happily ever after.

"Hmm, I sense this week's vocabulary words all have something in common," Mom said after

I read the story out loud to her and Dad.

"I wish Ms. Burland would be more *transparent* about it," Dad said. They laughed like it was a hilarious joke.

"May I go back outside now?" I asked. It made me grumpy that the girl in the story kept the cat, but I wouldn't be able to keep my kitten if I found him.

"One more time around the block," Mom said. "Then please set the table for dinner."

"No bringing any kittens inside, though," Dad reminded me.

"I know." I ran to the door with Banana bounding alongside me. She looked up at me with big, hopeful eyes. I felt a pang of guilt about leaving her inside again when I knew how much she wanted to go with me. With all the hours I'd spent looking for the kitten, I hadn't been spend-ing as much time with Banana as usual. Normally we had all our adventures together.

I hoped she didn't feel like she was being replaced by the kitten. No one could replace Banana. But finding the kitten felt like my responsibility—I'd been the first person to see him, and the first person to realize he was lost. If I didn't find him, who would? "I'm sorry, Banana," I said. "I wish you could come."

Banana sat and thumped her tail as if to say, *Pleeeeeeeease?* I hesitated. She thumped harder. I knew she could tell I was giving in.

"If we see the kitten, you have to promise to stay far away and not scare him," I said. Banana wiggled her whole backside in agreement. I clipped on her leash.

We looked left and right, up and down, and ahead and behind us as we circled the block. Banana sniffed the grass along the edges of the sidewalk and got excited when she saw a few squirrels, but we didn't find the kitten.

As we reached the Surely Shirley house, Banana perked up her ears, but it wasn't because of the kitten. She had spotted someone out in the garden.

Mrs. Shirley was sitting on a stone bench near the gazing ball, with a faraway look on her face. Banana and I kept walking until we were almost right in front of her, but Mrs. Shirley didn't seem to notice us.

I thought about the crying sounds my friends and I had heard yesterday, and Banana and I slowed to a stop. I had a hunch about why Mrs. Shirley was sad.

"Excuse me," I called to her. "Did you lose something?"

Chapter Eleven
Neither Here Nor There

Mrs. Shirley looked up. She seemed startled to see us there. "What? No, not something. Someone," she said.

Banana and I glanced at each other. "Was the someone a kitten?" I asked.

A sudden smile spread from the corners of Mrs. Shirley's lips all the way up to her eyes. She laughed. "He wasn't," she said. "He was my husband."

"You lost your husband?" Mrs. Shirley was still smiling, but Banana and I felt a little alarmed.

"Do you need us to help you look for him?" I offered.

She shook her head. "I don't mean that he wandered off. He died several months ago. I was just sitting here thinking about him, so your question caught me by surprise. That's all."

"Oh," I said. "I'm sorry for your loss." I'd heard Mom say that once to a woman at the library whose aunt had passed away. I wasn't sure what else to say about it.

"Thank you," Mrs. Shirley said.

Banana nudged me with her snout. "Do you miss him?" I asked. I wondered if that was why she'd been crying yesterday. If I ever lost Banana, I knew I would feel super sad.

"I do," she said. "Every day. Though in some ways I feel like he's still right here with me."

Banana's eyes went wide with surprise, and she took a small step backward. I knew she was thinking the same thing I was. "You mean . . . like a ghost?"

Mrs. Shirley laughed again. It was a nice laugh, one that bubbled and sparkled like fizzy ginger ale. "No, no. He doesn't haunt me," she said. "I meant it feels like he's here because of all the good memories. I'm so often reminded of him in nice ways. Especially when I'm out here in his garden . . . although it doesn't look nearly as beautiful as it did when he was alive. Edward loved taking care of his plants, but I'm afraid his green thumb never rubbed off on me."

Oh. So that was why the garden had changed so much. Not because of a witch. Of course.

I was glad the garden made Mrs. Shirley happy, even though it also made her miss him.

"He did make the garden beautiful," I said. "Banana and I always liked it."

Mrs. Shirley looked pleased to hear that. "I think as long as the people who loved him remember him, in that way he'll never truly be gone. He's still right here in my heart." She put one hand to her chest. "Does that make any sense?"

"Yeah." I nodded. "It does." I often felt like Banana was with me, even when we were apart, because I was always thinking of her. Banana leaned her weight against my leg, and I knew she agreed.

"Though I do get a little bit lonely now and then, so I'm glad you stopped to talk," Mrs. Shirley said. "I'm Samuella Shirley, by the way."

"I'm Anna and this is Banana. We live on the next street." I pointed.

"Yes, I think I know your parents," Mrs.

Shirley said. "Well, Anna and Banana, you've cheered me up considerably. Do come say hello again sometime."

"We will," I promised. Banana waved good-bye with her tail, and we headed toward home. We'd made a new friend, but not the small, furry one we'd set out to find.

Chapter Twelve
On the Same Page

After dinner, Banana and I curled up on the couch for reading time. Banana doesn't know how to read, of course, but she still loves books as much as I do, especially ones with pictures. Sometimes I read her a story out loud if I think it's one she might like. But I wasn't reading her the book about the witch. I knew it would be too scary. It was almost too scary for me.

Banana rested her head on my right knee and I propped the book open on my left, and turned to the next chapter. The girl was trying to trick the witch into releasing her from the enchanted cage. The witch leaned in close and squinted at the girl's face to test if she was lying. She put a bony finger under the girl's chin. Just then, the phone rang. The sound shocked me so much that I jumped and scared Banana.

"Anna, it's for you," Chuck called. I leaped off the couch and ran to answer. Someone might have found the kitten!

I took the phone from Chuck and cradled it to my ear. "Hello?"

"Hi, Anna," a voice said, and my hopes went *ka-thunk*. It was only Sadie. "Any news about the kitty?" she asked.

I pushed my disappointment aside. I was still glad to hear from my friend. "Isabel was right. He came back for more food. But I didn't catch him." I told Sadie everything else that had happened. I knew she and Isabel cared as much about the kitten as I did.

"You'll catch him tomorrow, for sure," she said. She sounded so certain, it gave me hope she might be right.

"Can you come over on Tuesday to practice for String Club?" she asked. "Isabel's invited too. I'll be at my dad's." I promised I'd ask my parents as soon as we hung up.

The next morning, I got up early to search for the kitten before school. I looked and looked near all the places he'd been before, sure that any second now I would see him. I was wrong.

By the time Chuck and I reached the school building, the first bell was ringing and Sadie and Isabel were waiting by the front door, bouncing on their toes. "No kitten," I said. Their faces fell. "But Dad said I can come over on Tuesday."

Isabel hooked her arm through mine, and Sadie did the same on the other side. They steered me toward our classroom.

"We're sorry, Anna," Isabel said. "But the kitten is out there somewhere. We'll find him soon."

Chapter Thirteen
Oh, Brother

"Did you finish that book yet?" Chuck asked as we walked home from school under the cloudy sky. "The spooooooooky one?"

He was teasing, but I ignored it. "Not yet," I said. "Almost." I only had three more chapters to go, but I was almost afraid to read them. I wasn't sure if it was going to have a good ending. Things were not going well for the girl and her brother.

"I can tell it's scary because you look like *this* when you're reading it," Chuck said. He bugged out his eyes and stretched his face into a ridiculous expression.

"Yeah, well, you look like *this* when you're *not* reading it," I said. I pushed up my nose and let my tongue hang out the side of my mouth. Chuck laughed.

"Hey, look," he said, but I waggled my tongue and crossed my eyes, trying to make him laugh some more. He grabbed my arm. "Anna. Look."

I let my eyes go back to normal and pulled in my tongue. As my vision cleared, I saw what Chuck had been trying to show me. Off to our left, just a few feet away, the little white kitten was at the edge of the sidewalk, giving himself a tongue bath.

I crouched down. *"Psst-psst-psst,"* I said, imitating the sound Isabel had made. The kitty looked up at me for a second, then returned to licking his leg. "Here, kitty kitty." I kept my voice soft and friendly. I didn't want the kitten to feel threatened and run. "Hey, pretty one. Are you lost?"

"I'll get behind him," Chuck said. He crossed to the other side of the street and made a wide half circle around the kitten, being careful not to frighten him.

"Psst-psst-psst," I said again. The kitten ignored me.

Chuck crept toward us, moving very slowly. Once he was only a few feet behind the kitten, he lunged and grabbed him around the middle.

The kitty screeched and flailed his paws in all directions, scrambling to get away. Chuck screeched too, and let go. The kitten bolted out of Chuck's grasp and leaped straight into my arms.

"He scratched me!" Chuck said, shaking his injured hand.

I cuddled the kitten close to my chest and held on tight. "Shhh, it's okay," I told the kitten and Chuck both. "I've got you, little kitty. You're safe now." The kitten nestled against me. He was even softer than he looked.

Chuck glared at us. "That thing's a ferocious beast," he said. "A vicious monster! He scratched me with his extra-sharp talons!"

I peered at the scratch on Chuck's hand. It was long and pink but not bleeding. "I think you'll recover. But you should wash that with soap."

"Hmph. Crazy attack cat," Chuck grumbled.

I stroked the kitten behind his ears, so he would know Chuck didn't mean it. "Thanks for helping rescue him."

Chuck puffed out his chest. "You're welcome." He paused. "Now what are you going to do with him?"

I looked down at the little kitten and up at the dark clouds. We heard a crack of thunder in the distance. Any minute now, a thunderstorm would start. We had to get moving, fast, or soon Chuck and I would be soaking wet, and so would the kitten.

"I can't take him inside," I said. "Dad's allergic. But I can't leave him out here. It's about to start raining, hard." As if to prove my point, the sky rumbled again, and a few fat raindrops fell from the clouds, splatting onto our cheeks and the sidewalk.

"Uh-oh," Chuck said. "Let's go."

Chuck turned on his heels and I followed behind him, moving as fast as I could without jostling the kitten. The kitten squirmed, but when I used one hand to pat his head, he relaxed.

Poor little kitten. I had to keep him safe and dry—I just had to! "Maybe I can hide him in my room until I come up with another plan," I said, thinking out loud. "As long as Dad doesn't go in there, the kitten probably won't make him sneeze."

"Probably not," Chuck said, but he didn't sound certain.

"I'll only keep him inside until the rain stops," I decided. "Then he'll be fine in the box outside.

But how will I get him past Dad in the first place?" I asked.

Chuck thought about it. "Tuck him under your sweater. You'll run upstairs and pretend like you have to go to the bathroom real bad, and I'll distract Dad until you come back down."

"You will?"

Chuck nodded, and I felt a surge of gladness at having him as my brother. If I hadn't been holding a kitten to my chest, I might even have hugged him. "Thank you," I said.

Chuck shrugged. "No problem. But that bloodthirsty little puffball owes me one."

Chapter Fourteen
Scratch That

When we got close to the house, I unbuttoned my sweater and tucked the kitten inside. I redid all the buttons except the one near his face. I wanted to keep him hidden but also make sure he could breathe.

Just as we reached the front door, the rain came pouring down. I shrieked and ran inside after Chuck. He shut the door quickly behind us, and we shared a big grin—that had been close, but we'd made it home just in time.

Banana danced at my feet, then stopped and

sniffed at the air. *Uh-oh*. Of course she could smell the kitten.

"Hello?" Dad called from his office on the other side of the house. Banana put her front paws up on my leg and pushed her nose closer to the kitten. I shoved her back down.

"Hi, Dad!" Chuck called back. To me, he whispered, "Go!"

"Hey, kiddos," Dad said as he came toward us. "I'm glad you're inside. It's raining cats and dogs out there, huh?"

By now Banana was running in excited little circles. She barked twice and tried to jump on me again.

Inside my sweater, the kitten twisted around. Luckily, my T-shirt was protecting me from his claws, but I had to get out of there before Dad noticed the lump. *"Shhh, shhh,"* I whispered to the kitten and Banana, trying to keep them both calm. "I'll be right back!" I said. I stepped over Banana and ran up the stairs, clutching the kitten to my belly. Banana followed, yelping at my feet.

"Banana, no!" I said, as sternly as I could while keeping my voice at a whisper. "Be quiet!"

Banana stopped barking, but she was still going crazy over the kitten. I knew she wanted to say hello to him, but of course I couldn't let her do that. I went inside my room and shut the door, pushing Banana out. "Banana, stay." Right before the door closed, I saw her ears go flat and her eyes look up at me, full of sadness and confusion. My heart lurched. "It's okay, girl," I said through the door. "I'll be out in a minute."

I unbuttoned my sweater and released the kitten onto my floor. He shook himself off, glanced at the door, then strolled over to Banana's basket where she sleeps beside my bed. He curled up on the soft, thick pillow inside it. For a second I felt guilty, knowing Banana wouldn't like the idea of the kitten taking her bed, but I had to admit he looked adorable there. And I was just so relieved he was safe.

"I'll be back in a few minutes," I told him. I slipped out the door, being careful not to let Banana inside, and ran to the bathroom to flush the toilet, so Dad would think that was what I'd been doing.

I walked downstairs, shrugged off my backpack, and gave Chuck a thumbs-up behind Dad's back. Chuck winked.

Dad turned around. "Where's Banana?" he asked, and I realized at that moment that she hadn't followed after me like usual. I heard her whine and scratch at my bedroom door. Dad's eyebrows shot up, and I knew he'd heard it too.

"She must, uh, want to take a nap in her basket," I said, even though we both knew what Banana always wanted was to be wherever I was. "Maybe I'll go up there with her. To read. And do homework."

Dad looked at me strangely. "Hey, about that kitten," he said. All the air whooshed out of my chest and my heart stopped beating as time held still. How did Dad know?

"Yeah?" I barely managed to squeak the word out.

"Two people called about it while you were at school," Dad said. "One person saw him running through a backyard on Antelope Ave, and another thought she might have seen him near Rosie's Bakery. But your kitten is white, right? It sounded like the bakery one was more gray."

"Oh," I said. So I hadn't been caught. I took a deep breath and exhaled my relief. But I still didn't dare look at Chuck. "Yup, he's white."

"He's unlikely to still be in either of those places now. But if you want, I'll help you look once the thunderstorm passes," Dad said. "I can't touch or go near him, but I can offer an extra set of eyes."

"That's okay," I said. I hoped it didn't show on my face that I knew exactly where the kitten was now: in my room. Dad wouldn't be smiling so kindly if he found out I'd snuck the kitten up there. I'd be in big trouble for breaking the rules.

Upstairs, Banana whined once more. "I, uh, have a lot of homework to get done," I said. "We can look for the kitten tomorrow." Misleading Dad like this felt terrible, but I was in too far now to turn back.

"Hey, Dad, can I show you this thing I learned in school today?" Chuck said. He tipped his head toward the staircase and mouthed, *Go!*

"Of course." Dad turned toward Chuck.

I mouthed *Thank you* to my brother and ran up the stairs as fast as I could.

Chapter Fifteen
Claws Out

Banana wagged her tail quickly and let out a yip when she saw me coming toward her. She really wanted me to let her visit the kitten.

I opened the door just wide enough to slide through it, and shut it firmly behind me, leaving Banana in the hall. I hoped she understood why I had to keep her out. I didn't want her to think I was choosing the kitten over her, but it wouldn't be fair to let her frighten him. I promised myself I would make it up to her later.

"Hi, kitty," I said softly. The kitten purred and wove around my ankles in a figure eight, lifting his back to rub it against me. I smiled and plopped down on the rug beside him. He was so skinny, I could feel the bones beneath his fur as I ran my hand across his back. I wished I could think of a way to bring some tuna to my room without Dad getting suspicious, but it was too risky. The kitten would have to wait until I could sneak him dinner.

The whole time I was petting him, Banana whined outside the door. I thought if I ignored her, she might give up and be quiet, but the whining only got worse.

I couldn't blame her. Banana wasn't used to being kept out of my room. We always did everything together. I would feel sad and jealous if she locked me out too.

"It's okay, Banana," I called in my most soothing voice. Banana whined harder and scratched at the door.

I panicked. If Banana kept this up, Dad would hear the noises and know something was wrong. If he came to investigate, the kitten would be discovered.

Even though the kitten was afraid of Banana, I had to let her in. Maybe they'd get used to each other and everything would be fine. Surely it would be better than all the scratching and whining.

I opened my bedroom door just a crack.

Banana immediately stuck her nose in as far as it would go. "Okay, Banana, I'm letting you in," I said. "But you have to promise, promise, promise to be good."

Banana blinked her agreement and dashed inside the room the second I opened the door a little wider. I heard a hiss behind me and realized my mistake: I should have gotten the same promise from the kitten.

Chapter Sixteen
Yip, Yap, Yikes!

The kitten hissed. Banana growled. *"Shhhhhhh!"* I warned them. "We have to be quiet!"

But Banana and the kitten didn't listen. They were frozen nose-to-nose in a supertense stand-off. Their whiskers twitched and their fur stood on end. It looked like any second now, either one of them might pounce. I had to do something before the fur started flying.

"Banana!" I stepped toward them. Banana kept her nose to the kitten's but glanced my way for just a second. The kitten seized his chance. He swiped at Banana's snout with his paw, then turned and dashed under my bed, meowing all the way.

Banana yelped and pulled back in surprise. It didn't look like the kitten had hurt her, but she'd definitely been startled. She shook her head, ears flapping, and ran to the bed to stick her nose underneath.

The kitten howled. Banana barked. This was a disaster.

"Banana, please! Kitty, hush!" I cried, but it was too late. I could hear Dad's footsteps coming swiftly up the stairs.

"What's going on in there?" Dad said.

"Nothing!" I said. But the doorknob was already turning.

Banana barked again as the door swung open and the kitten shot out from under the bed. I reached out and tried to grab on to Banana's collar but she moved too fast, chasing after the kitten as he leaped around my room, as crazy and springy as a bouncy ball on the loose. He jumped onto my dresser and scrambled across my desk, knocking over everything in his way. He sprang onto the laundry basket, spilling dirty clothes across the floor, and bolted for the door in a streak of white, escaping right between Dad's legs. Banana followed close behind.

"What on earth?" Dad said.

"Banana!" I screamed, pushing past Dad to run after them. Banana and the kitten flew down the stairs, boinged across the living room, and raced full-speed toward the kitchen. I had to catch them before they tore the whole house apart!

"Catch that cat!" I yelled to Chuck, who stood watching the commotion with his mouth hanging open and a half-chewed glob of potato chips inside.

"Anna! Banana!" Dad thundered as he ran down the stairs.

The kitten and Banana darted around me, just out of my grasp, and sprinted toward the front of the house. Just then, the front door opened, and Mom stepped inside. The kitten streaked past her, straight out into the pouring rain.

"No!" I shouted, and threw myself at Banana to keep her from following after him. I grabbed

her collar just in time, and held on tight. Mom shut the door and Banana gave up the chase.

Banana licked my cheek as I caught my breath. We looked up at my parents and Chuck. Dad's arms were crossed. Mom's hands were on her hips. Chuck still hadn't even closed his mouth.

I was in big, big, big trouble.

Worse, the little white kitten was gone.

Chapter Seventeen
Little Kitty, Big Trouble

My parents were so mad, they didn't even yell at me right away. They just sent me upstairs to start cleaning the mess while they discussed what they should do with me.

I didn't try to defend myself. I knew I'd messed up big-time. I went straight to my room, threw myself onto the bed, and burrowed my face in the pillow.

I wondered what my punishment would be. Maybe they'd lock me in an enchanted cage, or take away all my books, or throw me out into the storm. Whatever they decided, it couldn't be anything nearly as terrible as knowing that not only had I disappointed them, I'd also scared the kitten away. Now he was outside in a thunderstorm, getting soaked by the rain, running as far from Banana and me as he could get.

I didn't blame him. I would run away from me too, if I could. I'd wanted to save him but I had only made everything worse.

I felt a soft push against my hand that was dangling off the side of the bed. Banana nudged my palm with her nose and gave my fingers a little lick. I lifted my face from the pillow. "Oh, Banana," I said.

Banana sighed. She looked as sad and guilty as I felt. We both flinched as downstairs, Dad sneezed.

I heard a throat-clearing noise and looked up to see Chuck standing in the doorway. He had his hands shoved in his pockets and his shoulders up high by his ears. His eyes focused down at the carpet. "I'm sorry," he mumbled. "I shouldn't have helped bring the cat inside. I didn't mean to get you in trouble."

I shook my head. "It's not your fault. Or Banana's, either. I'm the one who made the bad decision."

Chuck looked around my room, and his lips twitched into a grin. "For such a small cat, he sure caused a big mess," he said. I almost smiled back.

Chuck picked up my knocked-over laundry basket and threw a dirty sock inside. "C'mon, Annabean. I'll help you clean up."

Chapter Eighteen
Unhappily Ever After

"Bad news," I told my friends on the playground the next morning. "I can't come over after school today. I'm grounded for the rest of the week."

"Oh no!" Sadie said.

"Yeah. I also have two extra spins on the chore wheel every Saturday this month." I took a deep breath and confessed the worst part: "And I think I may have lost the kitten forever."

Isabel's eyebrows pushed together with worry. "What happened?" she asked.

I filled them in on the rescue disaster and the lecture my parents had given me after dinner.

Mom said if I'd only told Dad about the kitten instead of sneaking him into my room, Dad would have helped set up a place for him in the garage. He'd have been safe there until we figured out what to do with him next. Instead, I'd put Dad in danger, and that had put the kitten in danger too.

I hadn't even thought about telling Dad, but of course he would have helped. In fact, after the lecture and the declaration of punishment, Dad had found four flashlights, and we'd all gone outside in our raincoats to search. Even Chuck went, and he hates the rain. But of course we hadn't found anything. The kitten was long gone.

"I bet he found someplace dry to spend the night," Sadie said.

"Yeah," Isabel said. "Cats are smart. And he

seems to have taken care of himself so far. But I still hope you'll find him again soon."

I hoped so too. But I was worried.

I worried about the kitten all morning long, from when Ms. Burland clapped twice to start the day, on through science, geography, and the spelling test. I worried about him more during String Club at recess, while Keisha showed us how to turn Cup and Saucer into the Star. Isabel and Sadie both got it right away, but I couldn't focus. The worrying made my insides feel as tangled and knotted as my string.

After recess, Sadie led the way to our favorite table in the cafeteria. When I opened my lunch bag, I saw that Dad had packed me an extra treat—both a box of raisins and a strawberry fruit strip. I knew it was a reminder that even though he'd been upset about what I'd done, he still loved me. I shared the raisins with Isabel and Sadie, and felt a little bit better. But then Ms. Burland walked by our table and I noticed her cute shoes. There was a puppy face on the toe of one foot, and a kitten face on the other. I looked away from the cat shoe and swallowed hard.

At silent reading time, I took out my book, grateful for the chance to get lost in a story about something else. I'd been right to worry about how the book would end, though. It wasn't a scary ending, but it wasn't truly happy, either. After she saved her brother, the girl saved herself, too, by tricking the witch into turning her into a butterfly. She defeated the witch and flew away, but she'd never be a human girl again. I liked that the girl had been brave for her brother, but it still left me feeling sad.

I closed the book and sighed. Isabel passed me a note. I opened it under my desk so Ms. Burland wouldn't see. *You okay?* it said.

Sad ending, I wrote back.

Isabel drew a frowny-face next to her reply. *Maybe you should write a new one.*

You mean, a new ending to the book? I asked. I tossed it onto her desk when Ms. Burland wasn't watching.

Isabel unfolded the note and gave me a shrug. *Why not?* she mouthed.

Huh. It wasn't a terrible idea. I took out my purple notebook with the three pony stickers on the front and grabbed my supersparkly rainbow pencil from its spot at the top of my desk. I tapped the pencil against my lip and thought about how to make things turn out better.

Maybe that didn't have to be the end of the butterfly girl's story.

Maybe there could still be a happier ending for the little lost kitten, too.

Chapter Nineteen
Pretty Please with a Kitten on Top

When the school day ended, I watched Sadie and Isabel get on the bus to Sadie's house. I knew my friends wished I could go with them too, but that didn't change the fact that they would be having tons of fun without me. Being grounded was as stinky as stepping in dog poo. I hated feeling left out.

I trudged down the sidewalk next to Chuck, stepping on every crack we came across. I didn't even care if it gave me bad luck. My luck was already terrible.

"Maybe the superstition is wrong," I said. "Maybe it's bad luck when a *white* cat crosses your path." But as soon as I'd said it, I wished I could take it back. I knew none of what had happened was the kitten's fault. It was all mine.

Chuck shook his head. "Nope. It's only black cats. But my teacher says sometimes you can choose to make your own luck." I thought about Isabel's idea to write my book a new ending, and how doing that had made me feel better. Isabel would probably like the teacher's theory. I bet Banana would like it too.

I jumped to avoid the next crack. Maybe it was time to change my luck, or at least snap out of being grumpy about it.

I took the yarn loop out of my pocket and wove it through my fingers. "Guess what the word of the day was today?" I said. I love the word of the day. It's one of my favorite things about being in Ms. Burland's class.

"Uh . . . 'boogers'?" Chuck guessed.

I leaped over another crack. "Nope. It was 'fad.' A fad is like a trend or a craze—something that gets really popular all of a sudden, out of nowhere."

"Like boogers?" he said.

I rolled my eyes. My brother was so predictable. "No, like String Club!" That was Ms. Burland's example.

"Yeah, I guess boogers aren't a fad because they're *always* popular," Chuck said with a smirk.

"You're disgusting," I informed him.

"Thank you," he said.

When we got home, I took Banana for a walk

and ate my half of the peanut-butter crackers Dad had put out for our snack. I snuck a little bite of one to Banana, too. She licked her lips and stared up at me like I was magic. She loves peanut butter even more than I do.

Chuck grabbed his baseball glove and left to play catch with his friend Erika. I wished for the millionth time that I had a friend in the neighborhood who lived in walking distance too. Not that I'd be able to play with one today anyway, since I was stuck at home being grounded. But still, it would be nice.

I wondered what Sadie and Isabel were doing now. I wondered if they missed me or if they'd already forgotten I wasn't there.

I was just starting to get sad and grumpy again, when the phone rang. "I'll get it!" I yelled. I ran to pick it up.

"Is this Anna?" the voice on the other end asked after "hello."

"Yes," I said, uncertain who it could be. The only adults who ever called me were Nana, Grumps, and Uncle Rob, but this didn't sound like any of them.

"This is Mrs. Shirley," the voice said. "I saw your signs about the lost kitten. I think I might have just seen him out in my garden."

I gasped. "You did?" I looked down at Banana to see if she'd heard that. Banana lifted her ears to listen to whatever Mrs. Shirley said next.

"He's not there anymore, but it seemed like he was going in the direction of Maple Street," Mrs. Shirley said. "Good luck, Anna. I hope you find him."

"Oh, thank you, thank you!" I hung up the phone and rushed after Banana, who was heading for Dad's office. Normally we're not supposed to interrupt Dad while he's writing, but Banana was right: This was an emergency.

"Dad!" I shouted as I pushed open the door. Dad looked up from his computer and raised both eyebrows at us. Banana was already spinning in circles. She was as happy as I was to hear the kitten was okay. "Dad, Mrs. Shirley saw the kitten!"

A slow grin spread across Dad's face, and I knew a pun was coming. "Well then *surely* you'd better go catch him," he said.

"I will," I said. "But Dad . . . I don't know if I can catch him by myself. It took two of us to corner him last time. And Chuck is at Erika's and you're allergic, but Sadie is with Isabel and Isabel is a cat expert."

"Hmm." Dad frowned.

I gave him my most pleading look. "I know I'm still in trouble, and I'm not trying to get out of being grounded. You can ground me for an extra month after this if you want. I'm just really, really worried about the kitten."

Dad sighed. "I know you are, kiddo. I know

how much you care about all animals, not just Banana, and I'm proud of you for that." I bit my lip and waited for the "but." Dad put his hand on top of my head. "You start looking and I'll call Sadie's father to see if they can help. You're still in trouble for what happened yesterday, but I'm willing to make a small exception for this."

I threw my arms around his middle and squeezed tight. "Thank you, Dad-o."

"You're welcome," he said. "Now go find that kitty."

Chapter Twenty
Stringing It All Together

"Psst-psst-psst," I called as I walked past the Surely Shirley house and down the block toward Maple Street. I ducked to check under each parked car, looked up into all the treetops, and scanned every backyard I could see. No kitten.

"Here, kitty kitty," I said. "Good kitty. Don't be scared." I wondered if cats have as good hearing as dogs. Listening is one of Banana's superpowers. She probably could hear me now, even all the way back at the house. Wherever the kitten was, I hoped he could hear me too.

"Psst-psst-psst," I repeated as I searched up and

down all of Maple Street for the second time. I tried to sound cheerful but with each step I took and each minute that passed, my mood sank lower and lower. "Kitty, kitty, kitty!" My eyes stung with tears of frustration. It felt like I would never find him.

Just as I was about to give up and head back, I heard a noise behind me. I turned and saw Sadie and Isabel running toward me. My spirits lifted like a kite in a gust of wind.

"Any sign of him?" Sadie asked when they got closer.

"No," I said. "I'm so glad you're here."

"We're going to find him," Isabel said. She gestured toward the notebook Sadie was clutching to her chest. "Sadie wrote down a plan." But as soon as the words were out of her mouth,

Isabel's eyes popped wide open and she pointed. "There!"

I turned and saw a flash of white disappear under a bush. "You found him!" I cried. Of course, we still had to catch him. But luckily, Sadie knew just what to do.

She grabbed my hand. "Let's spread out in a circle around the bush, so wherever he runs out, one of us will be there to grab him."

"Good idea," Isabel said. "And if he doesn't come out on his own, we'll lure him with this." She pulled a can of tuna from her pocket.

We approached the bush slowly, so the kitten wouldn't feel threatened. When we were positioned all around it, I crouched and peeked inside. The little white kitten blinked back at me. He was sitting in the center of the brambly bush, surrounded by sticks and leaves. He was too far in for us to reach in and get him. He would have to come out on his own.

Sadie called to him softly and held open her hands, so he could see there was nothing scary in them. The kitten didn't move.

Isabel pulled back the lid on the can of tuna. "Are you hungry?" she asked. "I brought you something tasty." The kitten's ears twitched, but he stayed put.

"Maybe you should hold out a taste of it," Sadie said. Isabel dipped her finger into the tuna and reached her hand slowly toward the kitten. The kitten sniffed a few times in Isabel's direction, but didn't accept the treat.

"Should we leave it and see if he comes out for it while we're not there?" Sadie asked.

I shook my head. "Then we might lose him completely."

Isabel agreed. "I wish there were a way to reassure him that we're friendly." She put down the tuna can. "We don't want to hurt you, little kitty. We just want to play!"

Play. That gave me an idea. I dug into my pocket and pulled out the string I'd been using earlier for String Club. Cats love playing with string, right? I dangled it near the bush to catch the kitten's attention. He suddenly looked very alert.

"Look, kitty," I said. I looped the string around two fingers, letting most of it dance back and forth through the air. The kitten stuck his head forward, watching. "Wanna play?"

I jiggled the string inside the bush, and the

kitten swiped his paw toward it. Isabel laughed. "It's working!" Sadie whispered.

I moved the string back and forth again. The kitten batted at the loose end. He moved closer, and I dragged the string along the ground, making it move like a mouse's tail.

The kitten jumped out of the bushes and pounced on the string. I didn't grab him—I knew I didn't need to. He was happy to keep playing with the string. I teased him with it, yanking it just out of his grasp, and he darted after it, making Isabel and Sadie say, "Aww."

I pulled the string toward myself and the kitten jumped into my lap, sticking his claws into the yarn. He tugged on one end while I tugged at the other and laughed. "He wants to join String

Club!" I scooped him up into my arms and stood.

"It's a new string trick—Catch the Kitty! You'll have to teach everyone at recess," Sadie said.

"That was way cooler than Cat's Cradle," Isabel agreed. "Great trick, Anna."

I grinned at my friends. They beamed back. "Thanks," I said. "I couldn't have done it without you."

Chapter Twenty-One
The Tail End of the Tale

I held on to the kitten tightly and we walked back to my house, where Dad had set up the cat bed and a saucer of milk in the garage. When the door was shut firmly behind us, I put the kitten on the floor and sat cross-legged beside him. Sadie and Isabel plopped down to play with him too.

"He's so sweet," Isabel cooed as he lapped up the milk. "I wish I could take him home with me. Mewsic would never get along with another cat, though."

"I know," Sadie said. "I can't believe neither of my parents will let me have a pet. I've begged and begged, but they both say no." Sadie's parents usually give her whatever she wants, but her dad travels too much for her to have a pet at his house, and her mom claims to only like animals "from a distance," though she's always been nice to Banana.

"What are we going to do with him?" Isabel said. "He can't stay here."

Sadie ran her hand along the kitten's back. He turned and pushed under her palm to demand more patting.

"Should we take him to Happy Homes?" she asked.

"Maybe," I said. It wasn't a bad idea. Happy Homes Animal Shelter was where I got Banana. It was a good place for animals to find new homes with families that would love them. But I didn't want the kitten to have to wait for the right person to find him at the shelter after he'd been on his own for so long. I wanted him to have a new home right away. Preferably one where I could visit.

"I know!" I said. "Let's ask Mrs. Shirley. Maybe she'd like a kitten."

Isabel's face lit up. "She did tell you she gets lonely sometimes. The kitten would be good company. And we know he likes spending time in her garden, since he keeps going back there."

"It's perfect," Sadie said. "I mean . . . if she says yes."

A few minutes later, we were standing on Mrs. Shirley's doorstep with the kitten in Banana's pet carrier, along with the can of tuna and an extra loop of string. I explained the whole story. "Would you like to keep him?" I asked her. "I think he'd make a good friend. And it's nice to have an animal to love." I was suddenly very nervous she might say no.

"Perhaps," Mrs. Shirley said. "But only on one condition."

My friends and I looked at one another. "What's that?" Sadie asked.

"If you agree to come visit and play with him," Mrs. Shirley said.

We quickly said yes. "Maybe even Banana can

come sometimes. I mean, once she and the kitten get used to each other," I said. After the kitten settled into his new home, I hoped he would see that Banana wasn't scary. I bet he and Banana could even become friends, too.

Mrs. Shirley smiled. "The kitty and I would love that."

"What are you going to name him?" Isabel asked as we helped bring him inside.

"Hmm. I'm not sure yet. Any ideas?" Mrs. Shirley asked. She cradled the kitten in the crook of her arm, and he purred the loudest I'd ever heard him.

"Well," I said. "You could always name him Surely. Like, S-U-R-E-L-Y."

Mrs. Shirley laughed. "Surely Shirley," she said. "I like that."

I scratched under the kitten's chin. He purred some more. "I think he likes it too."

Acknowledgments

A tail-swish of thanks to all the readers, librarians, and educators who have welcomed Anna, Banana, and me into their schools—especially Libby Morrison, who wrote me my first fan letter in the summer of 2015 and invited me to visit McKinley Elementary School, and the third graders in Mrs. Donnelly's class at Springfield Estates Elementary, who introduced me to their version of String Club when I spoke at their school last year.

A grateful purr to my agent, Meredith Kaffel Simonoff, in whose careful hands I never feel lost.

Thanks to the entire team at S&S BFYR, especially editor Alexa Pastor, who helped untangle all the strings; editrix emeritus Kristin Ostby, who suggested a kitten; and designer Laurent Linn, who always brings the cuteness. Hey, Meg Park: *meow.*

Thanks to all the friends who gave pats of encouragement along the way (especially Amy Jo Burns, who kept me well fed under deadline), and to my dog, Arugula, who helped with my research. A bouquet of catnip for Sophia, Anna, Erika, Jeremy, Emmett, Henry, my parents, and Jeff. A whisker twitch toward Pizzi, Sämpfli, Mewsic, Tremelo, and Bär.

Okay, Rooga, you may play with the kitty now.

And now, a sneak peek
at the next book in the series,
*ANNA, BANANA, AND
THE RECIPE FOR DISASTER*

Batter Up

"No, not the carrots!" my best friend Sadie said to the television. "Don't add those to the cake batter! Yuck!"

My other best friend, Isabel, shrugged at the screen. "I like carrot cake," she said.

"Yeah, but *chocolate* carrot cake?" Sadie said. "Blech. No thank you." We watched as the kid contestants on *The Batter-Up Bake-Off Show* grated three large carrots into the mixing bowl and poured in a cupful of chocolate chunks. Sadie wrinkled her nose.

"I'd try it," Isabel said. "What about you, Anna?"

"If Dad served it for dinner, I'd have to," I said. That was the food rule at my house: You eat what you're served, even if it's beets or brussels sprouts.

"True, but you're at my house now," Sadie said. "There aren't any rules like that here." There weren't any food rules at either of Sadie's houses. Both of her parents let her eat what she likes. And here at her dad's place, we're allowed to watch as much TV as we want, too, although usually we're busy with games or adventures.

Hanging out at my house is still the most fun though because there we get to be with my dog, Banana. But Banana doesn't mind if I go to

Sadie's or Isabel's, as long as I tell her all about it afterward.

"I'd still probably try it," I said, "if only so I could tell Banana what it tastes like."

Sadie shuddered. "Just let her taste it for herself!"

"Nope. Chocolate is really bad for dogs. Like, it's basically poison," I said. I was always super careful to keep chocolate out of Banana's reach. Even the thought of her eating some made my heart skip with panic.

Isabel nodded. "Cats too," she said. "We thought Mewsic maybe ate some once, and had to take him to the vet." Mewsic is Isabel's gigantic orange tabby cat. He's even bigger than Banana.

"What did the vet do about it?" Sadie asked.

"She gave him some medicine to make him throw up," Isabel said.

"Aw, poor kitty," I said, trying not to picture it.

"Yeah, but at least then he was safe," Isabel said. I couldn't argue with that.

"Oooh!" Sadie grabbed the remote and turned up the volume. "This is my favorite part."

It had been Sadie's idea for us to watch TV today—she'd really wanted us to see this new baking show. "Batter up!" she cried out, along with the whole TV audience. On screen, the two teams of kid contestants stepped up to the judges' plate to show off their final creations.

"Whoa, they sprinkled carrots on top of the frosting, too," I said, as that team gave the "pitch" for why their recipe invention should win. "They're really into this chocolate-carrot thing."

Sadie stuck out her tongue. "Gross."

"I like it," Isabel said. "It looks like a Halloween cake."

"Yeah, but Halloween is over." Sadie leaned back into the couch where we were sitting. "I think the other team should win. Zucchini-walnut cookies sound much better, even though it's still vegetables for dessert."

"I'd at least give the carrot team points for creativity," I said.

"Definitely," Isabel agreed. But the judges agreed with Sadie. They awarded the golden chef's cap to the other team.

"We should go on this show together," Sadie said, clicking it off with the remote. "We're a really good team."

"But we don't know how to bake!" Isabel said.

"So? We'll learn." Sadie tossed a throw pillow at me and I caught it. "I'm going to a cupcake-making party tomorrow after school, actually," she said.

Isabel perked up. "You're going to Monica's birthday party? Me too!"

"Cool!" Sadie said. She and Isabel beamed at each other.

I looked back and forth between them, feeling suddenly left out. "Who's Monica?" I asked. I didn't know Sadie and Isabel had a friend in common who wasn't me.